Weekly Reader Children's Book Club
presents

Half-As-Big

and the

TIGER

by BERNICE FRANKEL

pictures by LEONARD WEISGARD

FRANKLIN WATTS, INC.
575 Lexington Avenue • New York 22

Half-As-Big
and the
TIGER

WEEKLY READER
CHILDREN'S BOOK CLUB

In the forest there lived three deer who were brothers. The
eldest deer was big. The middle deer was just as big. But the
youngest was only half as big as his two brothers. And that is
what they called him — Half-As-Big.

Elder Brother was the strongest. He had the job of yanking down branches of juicy leaves for the family.

Middle Brother was the fastest. He had the job of running ahead to see if there was danger.

Half-As-Big? He was the wishingest; he wished he was big. He had no job at all — except answering to the name of Half-As-Big, which he didn't like a bit.

"Half-As-Big! Come eat your leaves," Elder Brother would bellow.

"Half-As-Big! Come follow me," Middle Brother would pant.

"Coming," Half-As-Big would sigh.

One day, when the three deer were exploring a new clearing in the forest, a great, fierce tiger suddenly appeared, and started to circle in on them like a noose.

Half-As-Big turned to
Elder Brother.
"Trample him, trample
him," he cried.
Elder Brother looked at
the rippling muscles of the
tiger. Elder Brother shook
his head.

Half-As-Big turned to Middle Brother.

"Race him, race him," he cried.

Middle Brother looked at the flowing leaps of the tiger. Middle Brother shook his head.

Half-As-Big had no one left to turn to — except himself. He took a deep breath, and called: "Ho! Tiger! Come here."

The tiger stopped. His tail shot up like a question mark. Could he trust this bold creature to be as helpless as he looked?

"What do you use your horns for?" asked the tiger.

"I shoot them out," said Half-As-Big, "as the porcupine shoots out needles."

When the tiger heard that, around he spun, away he dashed — as if one hundred porcupines were after him.

He was still running when he met a fox and told him what had happened.

"Half-As-Big cannot shoot out his horns," said the fox.

Back to the clearing the tiger stormed.

"Ho! Tiger!" called Half-As-Big. "Come and count the spots on my skin. See if I have as many as the snake swollen with pig."

The tiger stopped. His tail shot up.

"Why do you have so many spots?" he asked.

"Because," said Half-As-Big, "a spot appears every time I eat a tiger."

When the tiger heard that, around he whirled, away, away — as if one hundred porcupines and two hundred spotted snakes were after him.

Again he met the fox.

"Half-As-Big was born with those spots," said the fox.

Back to the clearing the tiger raged.

"Ho! Tiger!" called Half-As-Big. "Twice you ran away. This time, like the fearless skunk, I'm coming to you!"

And step after step after firm little step, Half-As-Big advanced toward the tiger.

The tiger didn't stop.
Or raise his tail.
Or ask a question.
He just whooshed around as fast as he could, away, away, away
— as if one hundred porcupines, two hundred spotted snakes,
and three hundred skunks were after him.

This time Half-As-Big thought the tiger would never come back. He kicked up his heels. He, Half-As-Big, had tricked a tiger! All by himself! All by himself! All by himself he had tricked a tiger!

"Ho! Elder Brother," he called. "Ho! Middle Brother."

"Coming, Half-As-Big," bellowed Elder Brother, from behind some trees.

"Coming, Half-As-Big," panted Middle Brother, from behind some bushes.

In ten leaps and a jump they were beside him.

Elder Brother looked at Half-As-Big with new respect.

"I didn't know you could think so quickly," he said.

"I didn't know it, either," said Half-As-Big.

Middle Brother looked at Half-As-Big with new respect.

"I didn't know you had so much courage," he said.

"I didn't know it, either," said Half-As-Big.

But just then the three deer heard a twig crack in the distance.

There, tearing toward them, was the tiger again!
Eyes ablaze!
Bristling with fury!
And this time the fox was
riding on his back!

"Ho! Fox!" shouted Half-As-Big. "You kept your promise to bring me a nice, fat tiger!"

When the tiger heard *that*, he just couldn't change directions fast enough. Oh, what a mighty double flip that tiger did. Even in the air his paws were running, and when he hit the ground he streaked off so fast it was hard to believe he really had been there.

But he had, all right —
for there in the tallest treetop,
where he'd been flung,
was the fox,
limp as a fur piece.

Again, Half-As-Big called his brothers from their hiding places:

"Ho! Elder Brother. Ho! Middle Brother."

"Coming, Twice-As-Smart," bellowed Elder Brother.

"Coming, Twice-As-Smart," panted Middle Brother.

The thinker of the family pranced for joy.
He was still only half as big as his two brothers.
But he was twice as smart!

After some years of evaluating children's books — as an editor of children's books, as the author of the weekly "Books for Children" column of the *Saturday Review* syndicate, in articles for *Town and Country* and other magazines — BERNICE FRANKEL finally followed a long-felt desire, and sat down and wrote a book herself. She hopes that children have as much fun reading HALF-AS-BIG AND THE TIGER as she had writing it. She intends to write other books for children. She lives in New York City.

LEONARD WEISGARD is well known as
an author of books for children and
as the illustrator of a wide variety of
books by other writers for children.
In 1947 he was awarded the Caldecott
Medal for THE LITTLE ISLAND, by
Golden MacDonald. He spent many
years in New York City, where he at-
tended school and later studied art and
the dance, while at the same time he
prepared to work creatively with children's books. He now lives in Connecti-
cut.